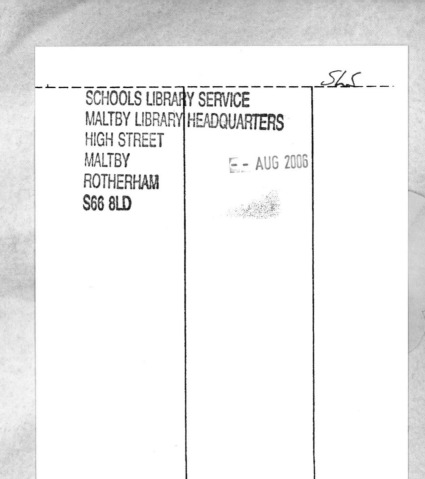

To S. V. C., good friend then and now
F. P. H.

First published 2003 by Walker Books Ltd
87 Vauxhall Walk, London SE11 5HJ

2 4 6 8 10 9 7 5 3 1

Text © 2003 Florence Parry Heide and Sylvia Van Clief
Illustrations © 2003 Holly Meade

This book has been typeset in Slimbach

Printed in China

British Library Cataloguing in Publication Data:
a catalogue record for this book
is available from the British Library

ISBN 0-7445-8060-9

That's What Friends Are For

Florence Parry Heide and Sylvia Van Clief

illustrated by Holly Meade

WALKER BOOKS
AND SUBSIDIARIES
LONDON • BOSTON • SYDNEY

Theodore the elephant
is sitting in the middle of the forest.
He has hurt his leg.

What a pity!
Today Theodore was going
to meet his cousin
at the end of the forest.

"What can I do?" Theodore says.
"My cousin is at the end of the forest,
and here I am in the middle of the forest.
And I have a bad leg, and I can't walk.

"I know what I'll do," Theodore says.
"I'll ask my friends for advice.
That's what friends are for."

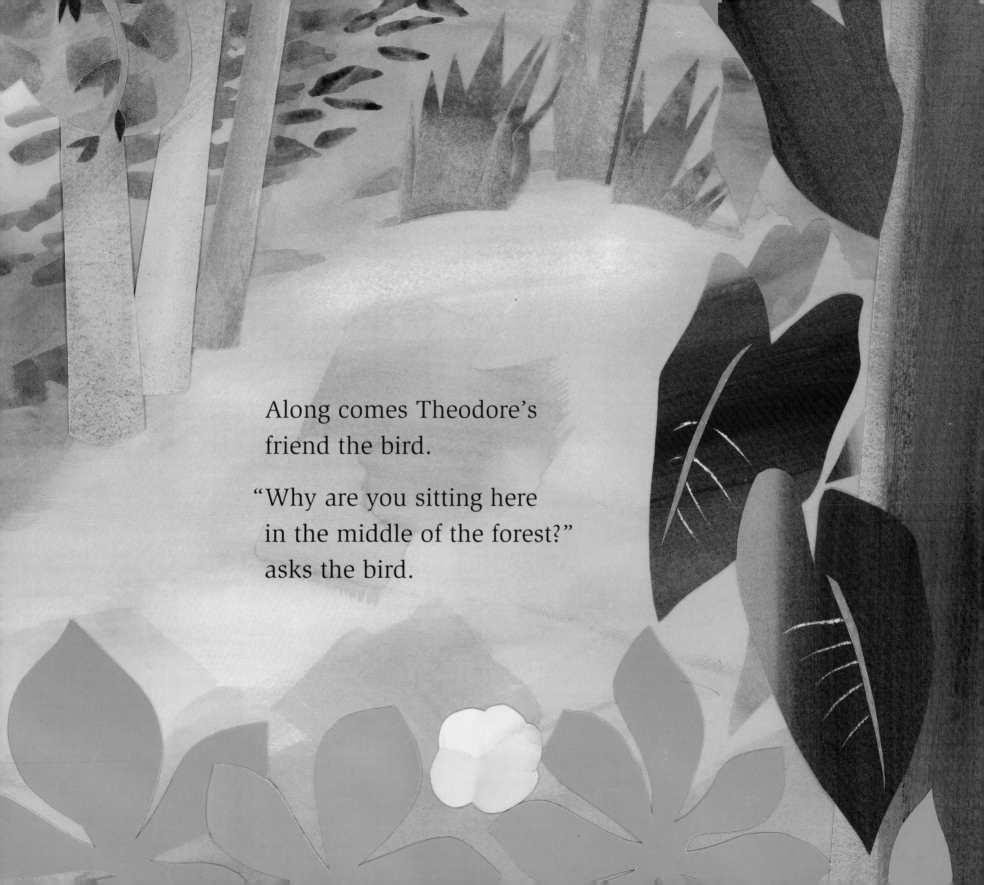

Along comes Theodore's
friend the bird.

"Why are you sitting here
in the middle of the forest?"
asks the bird.

"Because I have a bad leg,
  and I can't walk.
  And I can't meet my cousin
  at the end of the forest," says Theodore.

"If *I* had a bad leg,
  I would fly to the end of the forest,"
  says the bird to Theodore.

"It's nice of you to give advice,"
  says Theodore to the bird.

"That's what friends are for,"
  says the bird.

Along comes Theodore's friend
the daddy-long-legs.

"Why are you sitting here
in the middle of the forest?"
asks the daddy-long-legs.

"Because I have a bad leg,
and I can't walk.
And I can't fly.
And I can't meet my cousin
at the end of the forest," says Theodore.

"If *I* had a bad leg,"
  says the daddy-long-legs,
"I could still walk –
  because I have seven other legs."

"It's nice of you to give advice,"
  says Theodore.

"That's what friends are for,"
  says the daddy-long-legs.

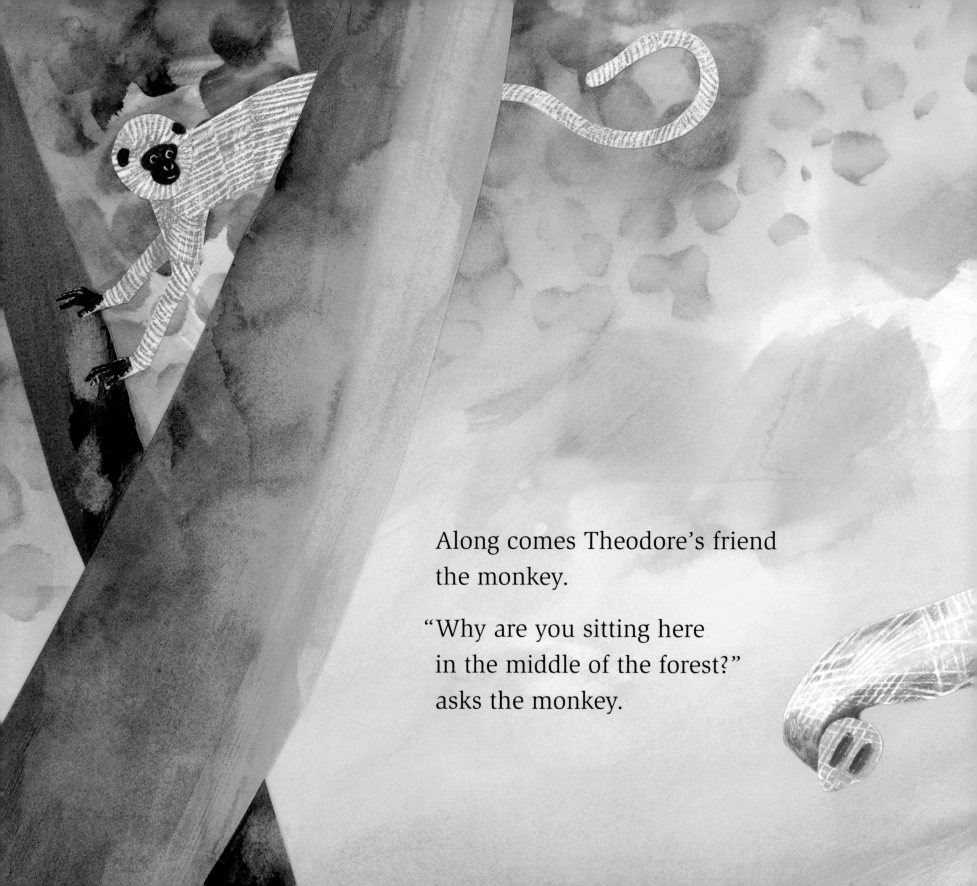

Along comes Theodore's friend
the monkey.

"Why are you sitting here
in the middle of the forest?"
asks the monkey.

"Because I have a bad leg,
and I can't walk.
And I can't fly.
And I don't have seven other legs.
And I can't meet my cousin
at the end of the forest,"
says Theodore.

"If *I* had a bad leg," says the monkey,
"I would swing by my tail from the trees like this."

"Well," says Theodore,
"I may have a very weak tail
 but I have a very strong trunk."

Theodore grabs the
tree with his trunk.

Crash!

"Well, anyway," says Theodore,
"thank you for your advice."

"That's what friends are for,"
says the monkey.

Along comes Theodore's friend the crab.

"Why are you lying down
in the middle of the forest?"
asks the crab.

"Because I have a bad leg,
and I can't walk.
And I can't fly.
And I don't have seven other legs.

"And I can't swing from the trees
by my tail (OR my trunk).
And I can't meet my cousin
at the end of the forest,"
says Theodore.

"If *I* had a bad leg," says the crab,
"I would get rid of it and grow another one."

"It's nice of you to give advice,"
 says Theodore.

"That's what friends are for,"
 says the crab.

Along comes Theodore's friend the lion.

"Why are you sitting here
in the middle of the forest?"
asks the lion.

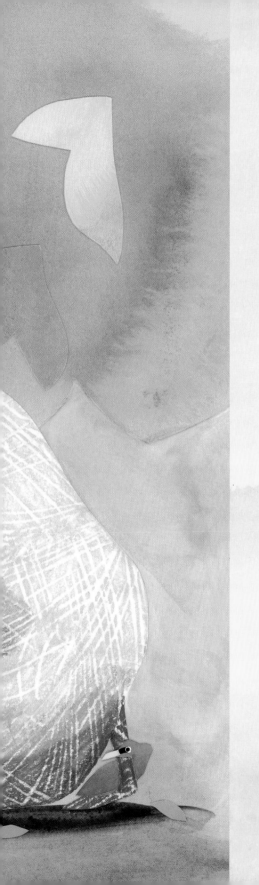

"Because I have a bad leg,
    and I can't walk.
    And I can't fly.
    And I don't have seven other legs.
    And I can't swing from the trees
    by my tail (OR my trunk).
    And I can't grow another leg.
    And I can't meet my cousin
    at the end of the forest," says Theodore.

"If *I* had a bad leg," says the lion,
"I would roar so loudly that
    everyone would come running
    to see what was the matter."

And he

roars.

"What's all the noise?"
 the opossum asks.
 He is hanging upside down by his tail.

"Theodore can't fly," says the bird.
"He can't get to the end of the forest
 to see his cousin," says the lion.
"We are giving him advice," says the crab.
"That's what friends are for."

"Nonsense," says the opossum.
"Friends are to *help*.
 Bring the cousin to Theodore."

So all the friends
go to find Theodore's cousin
at the end of the forest.

And they bring the cousin
to Theodore.

Theodore and his cousin
and all the friends are having a party.

"Thank you for *helping* me,"
says Theodore to his friends.

"That's what friends are for,"
say the friends.

To give advice is very nice,
but friends can do much more.
Friends should always help a friend.
That's what friends are for!